Mail Order Bride:
The Rejected Bride

By
Faith Johnson

Clean and Wholesome Western
Historical Romance

Table of Contents

Unsolicited Testimonials

By **Glaidene Ramsey**
☆☆☆☆☆ I so enjoy reading Faith Johnson's stories. This Bride and groom met as she arrived in town. They were married and then the story begins.!!!! Enjoy

By **Voracious Reader**
☆☆☆☆☆ "Great story of love and of faith. The hardships we may have to go through and how with faith, and God's help we can get through them" -

By **Glaidene's reads**
☆☆☆☆☆ "Faith Johnson is a five star writer. I have read a majority of her books. I enjoyed the story and hope you will too!!!!!"

By **Kirk Statler**
☆☆☆☆☆ I liked the book. A different twist because she wasn't in contract with anyone when she went. She went. God provided for her needs. God blessed her above and beyond.

By **Amazon Customer**
☆☆☆☆☆ Great clean and easy reading, a lot of fun for you to know ignores words this is crazy so I'll not reviewing again. Let me tell it and go

By **Kindle Customer**
☆☆☆☆☆ Wonderful story. You have such a way of showing people that opposite do attack. Both in words and action. I am glad that I found your books.

Chapter 1

For the last time, I stared at my aunt's barn, at the house I've lived in since I was four, after losing both my parents to illness. It felt almost unreal that I was leaving this home to go westwards to California, to marry a man I had never met. Still, I had little choice—this was to be my life now. And I had to accept it for what it was.

Although I was sad to be leaving, I also felt lucky to have this chance. I had been unsure what was going to become of me after my aunt's death. I had looked for work, but there was little opportunity in town for an inexperienced girl of only twenty. Then, to make matters worse, I found out that Aunt Charlotte owed several people money. It seemed she had been borrowing it, though I was not sure what exactly she had spent it on. It certainly was not on clothes or luxuries.

And so, when one of my aunt's friends brought a copy of *The Matrimonial Times* to me one day, I knew that I had to take a chance. I did not want to leave here—the only home I had really known—but neither could I stay. After perusing the ads, I found one that seemed well-written and kind. And after just a few more weeks and only a few letters, here I was—heading west as a mail order bride.

Sighing, I turned around to face the road that would take me to my future.

This house and property was someone else's now. Money had been scarce after my aunt's death, and selling the property was the only way. As I rode a wagon to the train station, I couldn't help but think of my aunt.

Aunt Charlotte had been without children. Her husband, my uncle, had died of yellow fever. It was quite a tragedy when my own parents had died too and I had to come and live with her. She had sold jams and jellies and sewing work at the town general store. She even worked the cattle that she had inherited from her husband. In many ways, she was a very impressive lady.

Even though she had taken me in, she never really treated me as her child. I was more like a tenant who paid her through the work that I did in the household. I had learned everything from her, and she made sure that I did my chores. When I was young, I used to cry in my room at night after having a tiring day. I used to wish my parents were alive back then. But at this point in my life, I was grateful to my aunt. Without her, I wouldn't have learned so many things, such as her beautiful handiwork and her cooking skills. Without her, I wouldn't have been such a hardworking woman myself.

I wondered what she would have said if she knew what I was going to do right now. I wonder if she would have approved. I liked to think so.

As I boarded the train for California, I realized that I might not ever come back here. I was leaving my childhood behind for an unknown place. My heart throbbed a little at the thought of never seeing my home again.

Tears stung at my eyes. I let myself feel the pain. I knew I had to leave these feelings behind to gain new ones. The train started to move, and as I went further away, leaving the familiar place, I realized that it would always be in my heart. Putting on a smile, I stroked away the tears of sadness.

***

After three days on the train, I finally reached my stop. Several people got down, and the station filled up quickly. I had no idea how to find the man I was meant to marry among all these people. I had sent him a photograph, though, and hoped that he would be able to find me. Feeling perplexed and a little worried, I made my way outside the station, pulling the heavy suitcase behind me. I tried to make myself easy to see, which was rather hard in the large crowd. And then, I saw him.

There, beside a wagon, stood the most handsome man I had ever seen. His auburn hair was swept inside a flat cap, and he wore a brownish jacket over his light-green buttoned-up shirt. He held a small piece of paper which looked to be a photograph, his eyes searching this way and that.

A look of recognition crossed his face on seeing me. He looked down at the photograph again, and then walked over to me.

"Alice Monroe?" he asked, his voice gravelly. I nodded my head. Was this the man I was to marry.

"Hello, I am Sam Conners. I am very happy to see you have arrived safely." He paused for a moment before looking towards his wagon. "I have something to talk to you about. We will talk in the wagon if you please."

Quietly, I took the seat beside him as he put my suitcase in the back.

Chapter 2

As we made our way through town, I wondered what he wanted to speak to me about. The tense built of his shoulders and the frown on his mouth pointed to something unfavorable, it seemed. Anxiety started building up in me. Already there was something unexpected in this altogether unusual plan.

"You already know that my earnings come from my claim on the gold in the river that flows through this small town," Sam started. I nodded my head in agreement with his words. I remembered he had mentioned that in his letters.

His eyes shifted downward for a moment, and I wondered what was wrong. "Well, in the last few weeks, I have not found any gold in my section of the river. I am afraid that the vein has been exhausted. In such times, I do not think I will be able to marry you, and furthermore, the preacher of this town is out on business. I am really sorry for this situation," he apologized, looking at me through the corner of his eyes. "I wrote you a letter explaining the situation, but I fear you must have left town before receiving it."

My heart fell a bit at the sound of his words. Did that mean he was not going to marry me? "I do not mind having a little less to go on. I am sure you can do something else as well." I tried to be encouraging. I didn't know where I would go if he rejected me. I had not received his letter, and even if I had, I knew I would still have come to meet him. I had no other choice.

"That is the problem here, Alice. I do not know any other job. I do have a few horses and a small garden, but I am not skilled in the trades like some men. And it would be some time before I felt ready to take on a wife, even if I were," he replied, looking me in the eye. "With my current income, I cannot even hope to start a family with you."

"I can help you earn money, and things would be better for us then. It's not like we have to get married right away. We can have some time to ourselves and figure this out." I was worried, yet I tried to be as strong and positive as I could be. This had to work.

"How will you, a woman, help me to earn money? There is nothing that you can do around here," he said sharply.

My heart squeezed at the thought of having to go back. This wasn't how it was supposed to be. He was supposed to welcome me into his life, especially since he had specifically advertised for it!

Ahead of us, I saw a small cabin perched on a hill. There was an equally small garden in front and a few horses and cows in the fenced area to the side. Just beyond the cabin flowed a river with glistening waters. Several cherry trees stood beside the river, with ripened fruits hanging on every branch. All in all, it was a lovely place, and made even more beautiful by the spring blooms.

As the wagon stopped, I had a sudden idea. "I can use your cherry trees to make jams, and I am also good at handiwork. I can make some lovely gloves and embroidered handkerchiefs after I have sold some jams. The cloth will come from that money."

Sam seemed surprised at my words. He looked towards the trees before he looked back at me, "You can't possibly be able to sell jams and your handiwork around here. The women are already good at that." But despite his warning, I could hear hopefulness in his voice.

In that moment, I flashed back to memories of my aunt. Although she had been a bit distant, she had always encouraged me to learn useful skills. She had not been afraid to try something new, including taking on cattle ranching. She had also taught me to never back down—a skill that had taken me this far already.

"You will see," I said firmly. "At least let's give it a try, and when the preacher comes back to town, we can be wed." I was determined to make this man want me, and I was going to do everything in my power to get him to see that.

After all, I had no other choice in the matter.

Chapter 3

"Such a pretty little thing," the elderly woman said as she gently touched my face.

"This is my mom," Sam introduced me to the woman who had opened the door to his cabin for us. "And Mom, this is Alice."

"Pleased to meet you, Mrs. Conners," I said, smiling at her. Sam was already out of the door, walking straight to his wagon. My suitcase was haphazardly placed before the front door. I looked towards his retreating back with a bit of dismay. My marriage—were it to even happen—did not seem to be off to the best start.

"Did my son make you upset already?" the woman asked with a good-natured smile.

Surprised, I turned my head towards her. "No, no, it's just that . . ."

I didn't know what exactly had made me upset about him. He was being truthful about his situation. I should accept his words and let him find someone else for me, but my heart just didn't want to go after someone else. And besides, could I even find another man to marry, and how would I live in the meantime?

The woman smiled kindly at me, her voice breaking into my unsettled thoughts. "I know that something has been bothering him, but don't worry. He decided it was time to marry, and Sam is not one to take things lightly. He can be rash sometimes, but don't take it to heart. He will come around. Besides, who can resist such a beautiful girl as you?" she chuckled, making me blush at her words. "Let me show you to your room so that you can freshen up. We can't have you share my son's room just yet."

I smiled and followed her. Maybe there was a chance for a life for me here after all.

***

"You make such delicious food that I couldn't help but eat a little too much." Mrs. Conners said as she finished her dinner. She smiled happily as she patted her belly.

"I am glad that you like my food, Mrs. Conners," I replied, taking the dishes to the sink. Hopefully, Sam would too. But so far, I had not seen him since he had brought me to the house.

Eliza stood and walked over to me. "You don't have to do the dishes too. You have made dinner, and that's enough work for you today. You should be resting, young lady, after such a tiresome journey," she said as she tried to push me away from the dishes.

Placing my hands on her shoulders, I gently moved her away, guarding the dishes with my back. "You have worked so hard for so many years, Mrs. Conners. You can go to bed early tonight. I can handle it here." I was determined to show them all how much I could add to the household.

"Please, child, call me Eliza and not Mrs. Conners. You can call me Mother, too, if you want. I would like that very much," she said, clutching my upper arm reassuringly, her eyes warm. Her words almost made me cry. I had never been able to call anyone Mother after my parents had died. I just nodded my head at her words, not trusting my voice to not break. If Sam was going to be distant and unsure if he wanted me, I was happy at least to have his mother to rely on.

After Eliza had gone to bed, I washed up and cleared up everything, keeping just a single bowl and a plate full of food. Sam still hadn't returned from the fields, and he hadn't had dinner. I wondered if he was avoiding me, and decided it was very likely that he was.

I sighed and pulled a chair up near the fire. Though the spring days were warming here, the nights were still quite chilly. I was happy for the warmth of the fire and the comfort of its gently flickering flames.

Taking out a few handkerchiefs I had brought with me, I sat down to begin embroidering them. I was glad I had brought some supplies with me, and I was determined to show Sam that I could help earn some money. I became quite lost in the pleasant task, and it was another half an hour before the front door opened and Sam walked in.

Quietly, he made his way to the table and stared down at the covered plates and bowls. He seemed not quite sure what to do with them.

"I kept some dinner for you. You can have it if you are hungry," I said as he glanced in my direction.

"You waited up for me?" he asked as if he was surprised by my gesture. He smiled, and I felt a little burst of pleasure.

I nodded. "Yes, I thought that it would be nice for you to have someone while you eat. I asked your mother to go to bed while I did some sewing," I confessed, taking up my sewing again. I hoped he would not turn me away.

Sam sat down at the table, taking the plate and bowl. "The food looks delicious." He took a spoonful of the stew and smiled. "And I must say that it tastes great too."

"Thank you," I replied quietly, looking at him. There was silence between us as he finished his dinner while I finished my sewing. Though I would not have minded some conversation, I was happy enough that he seemed to enjoy my cooking.

As I stood up to clear the plates when he was done, he suddenly called out, "Alice."

My eyes found his thoughtful ones instantly, and I felt a little leap in my heart.

"I apologize for being so harsh to you this morning. I shouldn't have put the news to you like that. I am just quite worried about what I will do for money now, and I do not know how to solve it. I do not want your life to be wasted because of my situation," he confessed.

Almost without thinking, I reached out and took his hand, squeezing reassuringly. Sam looked towards me, but he did not pull his hand away. I took that as a good sign, and decided to take a chance.

"Don't worry about me. I will be content to live with whatever you could make, and I have started my own venture that I spoke to you about. I would be glad if you could bring me some jars from the general store tomorrow."

"I will do that," he said, surprising me a little. "I have some business in town, and in the meanwhile, you could look at your jars and other necessities." Then with a gentle squeeze, he released my hand and smiled.

As he walked to his room, I heaved a sigh of relief. I just may be able to make a home here, after all.

Chapter 4

"I will be ready to head into town soon, if you still want to go," Sam said. "I just have a few things to tend to in the barn first." He smiled, then stepped out the front door.

"It is refreshing to see a young man trying his hardest to be good to his lady," Eliza chuckled. She seemed so amused. If only she knew that her son had denied marrying me, maybe she wouldn't have called me *his* lady. From the way Eliza spoke to me, I had decided Sam had not told her about his gold claim drying up, as it seemed maybe she was not aware of it. Maybe he did not want to worry her. And anyway, it was not mine to tell.

"I was thinking of telling him to go on his own. He can bring me the jars that he thinks are the best," I replied, reaching into the washing basket. Eliza and I had been hanging up the clothes I'd washed that morning, and I did not feel right leaving her with the chores still undone.

Suddenly, she caught hold of my hand, her face serious.

"You would do no such thing. You are going to go with my son to the town and get whatever you need. Am I clear to you?" she asked, her rather kind face taking on an unfamiliar look.

"But the housework . . ." I tried to say, but she shook her head.

"My old bones still have the strength to get everything done with expertise. Please go and spend some time with the man that you are going to spend your life with. You need to get to know him as soon as possible.

It is important if you are to marry him," she pressed. "Now, go."

Her slight push got my feet to move on their own. I realized she was right, and I needed to my part to make this marriage work. Quickly, we hung up the rest of the washing, just in time to spot Sam coming around with the wagon.

"I am glad you are coming with me," he said, helping me into the seat beside him. The wagon bumped along the way towards the town, and we talked easily of inconsequential things such as the weather and his plans for the barn. Neither one of us mentioned the gold, and for that moment, I was glad. I knew it was a sore subject with him, and I did not to ruin our first real time together.

"What did you bring in that basket of yours?" he asked, gesturing to my lap.

Looking down, I brought out one of the handkerchiefs that I was working on last night. I had finished ten of them, and this was one of my favorites. He took it in his hand, studying the colorful embroidery with an impressed expression.

"This is what you were sewing last night?" he asked as I nodded my head, taking it from him. Folding the cloth, I placed it into my basket again.

"Where did you learn to embroider like that? My mother used to be a part of a sewing club for ladies, but I have never seen anyone make such beautiful designs before." He looked over at me and smiled, and I noticed how green his eyes were.

"My aunt used to sew. She taught me everything that she knew," I said, with a tinge of sadness in my voice. Sam noticed my change in mood, and I saw it reflected in his face.

"Where is your aunt now?" Sam's eyes were studying me now, trying to decipher what I was thinking. I had never had a man care about me like this, and I decided to tell the whole story. After all, that was why his mother had encouraged me to come along in the first place.

"My mother and father died when I was four. My aunt Charlotte was all that I had. She taught me a lot of things, like this embroidery, and I don't think I truly appreciated them until now." My eyes teared up at speaking these thoughts out loud. Charlotte had not been a mother to me, not precisely, but she had taken care of me, and she was the only family I'd had after my parents' death.

There was silence between us for quite a moment. I only dared to look at Sam when I could finally trust my face again. I was glad I had told him the truth, but I did not want to burden him with troubles so soon in the relationship.

"I remember when my father died," Sam said, surprising me. "I felt such a hole in my life, I wondered how it would ever fill. And then I realize, it doesn't fill. You just get used to the hole, and it gets smaller. Your pain moves aside over time to make room for life again."

I look at him, impressed by his depth of thought. "Thank you," I said. There was much more to this man than I had anticipated, I realized. I wondered how much more there was.

We reached the town soon after, and Sam stopped the wagon before a store.

"I will go and find new pans while you can check out Boone's store over there for whatever you need. If he asks for money, just tell him that I will pay for it or you can just wait there and I will come and get you. They all know me here," he explained and I nodded.

I watched as he made his way with sure footing towards the blacksmith's.

My heart squeezed a little as he walked away. Then, taking a deep breath, I entered the shop he had pointed me towards.

Chapter 5

The store was empty when I entered. A man, almost the same age as Sam, was behind the counter. His dark hair fell on his temple as he wrote something on his pad with concentration. There was a crook at the bridge of his nose, showing that he might have been rowdy in his younger days.

Deciding not to disturb him, I went on my own to find the jars that I needed. They were at the very back of the store. Some of them had designs on the glass, which gave me an idea. Picking up twenty, I made my way to the front.

The man was still bent over the pad. Frustration was evident on his face. Unable to control my curiosity, I looked at the pad and noticed numbers written on it.

"I don't understand what I did wrong. This is just not making sense…"

I peered closer and noticed the mistake. I had always had a head for numbers, which my aunt made sure to encourage. Perhaps if I had helped her manage her finances, she would not have died in debt as she did.

"I think you counted it wrong here." Without thinking, I pointed out his error. The man's eyes lit up with realization, and once he had corrected that, the total on both the pages matched.

"Thank you—" He looked up at me and stopped in the middle of his sentence. He was about my age, and the way he looked at me made me blush.

Looking away, I placed the jars on the counter. "I want to buy these, please."

He took them and started packing them up. "I haven't seen you around here. My name is Boone Carson. I own this store. What is your name, ma'am?"

"I am Alice Monroe. It is nice to meet you, Mr. Carson," I replied.

"Thank you so much for helping me out with that calculation. Sometimes, I can sure be a little forgetful." He chuckled quietly as I smiled at his words. "Where are you staying?"

Before I could reply, a man's voice came from behind me. "She is staying with me at my house." The voice was gruff, and it startled us both.

Boone Carson and I looked towards the voice to find Sam standing there. Something was glinting in his eyes—some type of emotion I hadn't seen before. I took a step back unconsciously, even though Boone and I were doing nothing wrong.

"Really?" Boone looked more interested in me now. "She is new here, I take it? Is she a relative of yours?"

"She is staying with me. I think that is all that needs to be said on the matter," Sam spoke as he came to stand by me. I couldn't help but look at him with wide eyes. Why would he not tell the full truth, that I was here to marry him? Was he still not certain he wanted me? And could he not see the way Boone was looking at me?

"I must say your acquaintance is a beauty with brains. She helped me solve my problem. I wonder if perhaps you would like to go for a walk sometime?" he asked me. I looked towards Sam, and he just looked back at me with an expression I could not read. I realized he was waiting for me to answer, and so I did.

"I thank you for your kindness, Mr. Carson," I said, rejecting his offer politely, "but I am needed at the ranch." I opened my basket to place the jars in it. My eyes fell on the handkerchiefs, remembering that I had brought them to sell, and I pulled them out for him to examine. After Sam's reaction, I was ready to cut the visit short, but I told myself that making some money for the ranch was more important than a moment's discomfort.

"I do have one thing to ask," I said. "Would you like to check these handkerchiefs? I made them myself." With slow fingers, I handed them over to the man behind the counter. His eyes were wide as he ran his fingers over the birds and flowers and other designs that I had made on the cloth. Sam, I noticed, had stayed nearby but off to the side, not speaking.

"You made them yourself? I have never seen such beautiful designs," Boone said with appreciation in his voice. "I will take them, and I will pay you a dollar and fifty cents for three. Is that acceptable to you?"

"Yes, it certainly is." I smiled, feeling very thankful to my aunt. Though she had been strict in some ways, she had also prepared me for the world. Boone took out the money from his cashbox and handed it to me as I handed over the hankies to him. "And perhaps I can bring by some jam in the next few days? I plan to make some from the trees and bushes that grow on Sam's land." I looked at Sam with a smile as I said this, but he looked distracted and did not smile back.

"As I said, you are a woman of beauty and brains," Boone said again. Though his words were kind, I felt a bit uncomfortable under his gaze. "I would be happy to assess your jams."

But before I could speak, Sam took me by the arm. "We should leave now. I have something to do after this," Sam said roughly, already turning towards the door. The tone of his voice caught me off guard, but I was not terribly surprised. I'd seen the way he had been looking a Boone.

Boone seemed to have not noticed the tension in Sam's voice—or else he did not care. His eyes had not left me, and he said, "I look forward to seeing you again, Alice."

"Sam and I will bring the jams by soon," I said, then followed Sam out the door.

As I came out of the store, I saw the terseness in Sam's shoulders and his quick pace. I couldn't keep up with him by walking and had to resort to a fast jog.

As we sat down in the wagon, I gently prodded for an answer. "Is there something wrong, Sam? You look a little tense." I wasn't sure how much to push him, but I wanted him to know that I cared.

"It is nothing for you to be concerned about," he said a bit coldly. I flinched at his words. I knew he was probably upset about the attention Boone had paid me, but I had refused his offer, after all. And Sam had not been clear on our relationship, which was no help at all. Of course, I had asked him about the handkerchiefs and the jams, but that was business, and it was for both of us—and for the farm.

The rest of the ride back to his house was silent and tense. Neither of us spoke a word to each other.

Chapter 6

It had taken me the next three days to get everything ready for the jams that I planned to take to the general store. We were supposed to go to town today and see if Boone Carson would buy them like he had the last batch.

I had been nervous about the next meeting with Boone, but even though Sam had seemed very disturbed by the interaction with Boone the other day, he had also seemed to have gotten over it. We had even taken time to have a picnic just past town, in a lovely meadow. It had been nice to talk and wander through the wildflowers, and we had picked a lovely bouquet for Eliza. I told him some tales about living with my aunt, and how much she had helped me after my parents died. He, in turn, had talked about his dream of owning a large ranch, but then he found gold on his land and began to dedicate all his time to panning it from the river.

"I wonder," he had said, "at all the paths we get to choose from in our lives. We know what is at the beginning of the path, and we know what we hope for at the end. But we never really know where our choices will lead us."

"I agree," I had said. "I did not know I would be a mail order bride until that choice appeared in my path. And I did not know how much my aunt's teachings would help me in my life." I had wanted to say that I had not expected my path to lead to Sam, a kind and generous man, but I was a little afraid of his reaction. Even though neither one of us had mentioned marriage—it still seemed to make him uncomfortable—I knew we had some time. After all, a real decision did not need to be made until the preacher showed up.

After returning to the house, we'd had a lovely meal that truly gave me hope for the future, and I went to sleep with the sense of something precious just waiting to be discovered.

The morning was warm and sunny, and I decided to go and pick some more cherries for my jams. The cherry trees by the river had the biggest bounty of fruits that I had ever seen. It almost felt like their stock never diminished. As I went to pick up my fill for today, I noticed Sam sitting by the river. He held two empty pans in his hands.

Those were the ones he had brought from the store a few days back.

Quietly, I made my way towards him, down the hill. "Sam, can I get you anything?" I ventured. He looked sad and worried, and I knew he must not have found any gold today. I wanted to help him somehow, but I was not sure exactly how. My money from the jams and handkerchiefs might help the farm, but they would not help the way Sam felt about his gold claim.

He shook his head without looking at me. "No, I was just finishing up here. We have to go to the store, don't we? Just get ready for that," he said, standing and heading towards the house.

I could only sigh and follow him. Clearly, he was still bothered by the fact that his gold had run out, but I couldn't help him if he kept pushing me away.

***

The next few days passed by quickly. My idea of jams and handkerchiefs had been a success, and a handsome amount of money came from the sale of them and my handiworks. We were able to make some repairs on the ranch, and I bought a nice new set of gloves for Sam's mother. She had been very supportive of the whole enterprise from the beginning, and I was terribly grateful to her.

I was at the general store dropping off my latest batch of jams while Sam lingered in the front. He always came with me, but he tended to avoid Boone, I had noticed. I did not mind, as long as Boone acted appropriately while we chatted.

"I wonder if you could make any apple butter? I love that—my mother used to make it for us," Boone said, taking the new jars of jam from me.

"Sam doesn't have apple trees at his house. But I can make you some if you could provide the apples. You are my most loyal buyer after all," I said with a smile.

Boone smiled back. "Excellent. But I will not sell you the apples—I will give them to you. I can't ask you to pay when you are doing me this favor."

"It is no trouble at all," I assured him.

Boone looked at me again. "You truly are a remarkable woman, Miss Alice."

I felt myself begin to blush, and stepped back. "I must go now. Sam has been waiting for me for some time now." With that said, I made a small bow before making my way out of the store. Sam looked towards me as I approached.

"Are you ready to go?" he asked, and I nodded my head. As we boarded his wagon to return home, he glanced toward the apples in my basked. "Did you get new ingredients for your jams?"

"In a way. Boone asked me to make him some apple butter, and he gave me the apples for it. It just seemed like the polite thing to do, since he has been so helpful with selling my crafts."

Sam went quiet, then spoke. "You two are getting along very well, it seems."

"Well, he has been quite gracious, as I said." I spoke cautiously.

We continued down the road a ways before Sam spoke again. "The preacher is still not back, as you know, and I have heard he is delayed. He broke his leg and is staying in Sugar Gulch until it mends. So that gives you some more time."

"More time for what?" I asked, though I was afraid I knew where this was going.

"More time to change your mind, if you have decided I am not the man for you. Because I must be honest, Alice, I do not think I will ever be in the position to marry. You are working very hard, and I do appreciate that, but I am not the kind of man who could be happy having his wife take care of him in that way. I am meant to be the provider, not you."

I stayed silent, unsure how to respond. I could understand how he felt, but I still felt he was being silly. But of course, I could not tell him that.

He let out a heavy sigh, then said, "I just wonder if you would be more happy with someone like Boone."

I did not answer him—I knew it was useless—and we continued home without speaking again.

Chapter 7

Three days after the wagon incident, Eliza came to speak to me. I was sure she could sense the deep tension between Sam and me. For my part, I had been clueless as to what to do regarding his feelings towards me and us getting married. I had not brought the subject up again, and I was not even sure if I wanted to keep taking my goods to the general store to sell—even though I knew we needed the money. Was that just making things worse?

"What is going on between you and Sam?" Eliza asked as I was washing the dishes in the sink. Her hands were on her hips, and her face showed concern and kindness. Sam had just gone out after breakfast to whatever he did during the day.

"Nothing is going on between us." My voice was quiet.

I heard Eliza sigh behind me. "Did you two fight? Because I am no fool. I can clearly see that you two aren't talking. The moment you two are in the same room, I feel like I am going to suffocate with the amount of unshed feelings," she explained.

I was grateful for her concern but wasn't sure how much I should say. After all, this was between Sam and me. I continued to wash the plate I was holding but then could not contain my feelings anymore. My breathing came out haggard, and tears began to flow down my cheeks.

Eliza was instantly by my side, patting my back and trying to calm me down. "I will have his hide if he has hurt you in some way. I know that boy can be very stubborn at times. Tell me, what did he do?"

We sat down on the couch, and I poured out everything that had happened between Sam and me.

"I really think Sam doesn't want me here. I feel like he hates me and is annoyed by my existence, like it reminds him of how his gold strike is failing. Why else would he want to get rid of me? He said he is afraid he cannot support me, and even suggested I would be happier with Boone Carson, the man I have been selling my goods to. But I don't want to be with Boone. I want to be with Sam." Sniffling, I finished my explanation. I was glad to have gotten it off my chest, and felt a little better already.

Eliza shook her head kindly. "I do not think my son hates you. He is a man of few words, and he keeps a lot of his problems to himself, but I am certain he doesn't hate you. He really cares about you, and that's why maybe he doesn't want you to stay here. He wants you to have a better life with Boone. That man is the owner of the general store in town, and nothing can really go wrong with his business. Sam's gold claim is more of an uncertain situation."

"I never said that I wanted someone who had stability," I said with a sigh. "I am willing to work with Sam and help him with the household. My sewing and jams are doing well. I don't know why he won't just let me help."

"That is the problem, my child." Eliza sighed, a rueful smile on her face. "Men are often like that. They think that running the household is their duty. No matter how forward-minded they might be, they would always think that taking care of their woman is their responsibility. When they are unable to do so, they think that they are a failure. I believe my son, who is a very proud man, is no different. He feels that you would be better off with someone who could be a better man than himself. It's a matter of his male ego, his proud self."

"I know," I said. "He did admit that in the wagon. But I had really hoped he was just feeling upset. But now, thinking about how he has looked at me and Boone when we were talking, I know that has been bothering him more than I wanted to admit."

I rubbed my eyes and took a deep breath, to calm myself down. Why was I trying so hard for a man who doesn't even understand me? Did he really care about me at all? But if he didn't, what else was there for me to do? I didn't want to marry Boone—I didn't even know him. I didn't know Sam either, for that matter, but at least I knew him better than Boone, and what I had seen, I had liked—mostly.

"Then what should I do?" I asked quietly, staring down at my lap.

"You do nothing," she answered calmly. I spun my head so quickly to look at her that I almost stumbled.

"But—" I tried to explain. *She couldn't be serious,* I thought to myself.

"There are no buts and ifs at this point. Let me tell you another secret about men. I have learned through my long-lived life that you can never make a man do something. You can change a woman, but you cannot really ever change a man unless they want to. You only have the choice of waiting for him to come around, or you can leave this situation. Do you want to leave?" She spoke very calmly, but her eyes were serious. I paused for a moment to think and reflect on my days here with Sam.

I thought of all the times that Sam had been kind to me, the times when I had relied on him for judgment while I had been here. I also thought of Eliza, who had taken care of me like her own daughter. Then I thought of trying to live on my own, with no money or marriage prospects and only my talents with jam-making to sustain me.

"I don't want to leave," I said. I realized that even if Sam didn't see me like I wanted him to, I still believed he could. I felt sure I could convince him to allow my help, and we could start over again, somehow. I realized he was someone I deeply admired and someone with whom I wanted to build my home. Someone who I *loved*.

When had I started loving him? I wondered.

Eliza smiled and reached out for my hand, giving it a quick squeeze. "I am glad that you decided to stay. I have taken a liking to you. I would love my son to finally see your worth and to come around. He will be missing out on someone who will be good for him if he rejected you," she said.

She got up from the couch slowly, then spoke again. "I know things have been hard for you here, but trust me. I truly believe they will get better. Just give Sam some time. Don't give up on him."

She nodded, then walked outside to go tend to the afternoon chores. I couldn't help but stare after her. Wisdom did come with the ages if you were willing to take in life's lessons. Eliza was one of those women who had taken those lessons and had applied them to her own life. I felt so much lighter after my exchange with her, calmed and soothed. Maybe there really was no use in keeping everything in, trying to shoulder every pain by yourself.

I just wondered when Sam would understand that.

Chapter 8

The next few days passed quickly. I kept making my jam and working on the handkerchiefs when I could, but I also had decided not to go into town anymore—at least for a little while. Now that I knew how strongly Sam felt about Boone, I had decided it would be best if I did not see him for a while. I missed the money, but maybe I could find another way to sell my handicrafts.

Right now, I decided to keep my focus on Sam and the house. I remembered Eliza's words, and knew I needed to give Sam and me a chance. I would do that for the both of us.

For Sam's part, he also seemed to enjoy having me around, though he did not speak of it. He was a little more talkative during meals, and I was pretty sure he was smiling more. Often, my mind went back to the picnic in the meadow, when I had enjoyed a glimpse of the future we could have. I kept hoping we would have another chance to slip away, but the farm was keeping us both quite busy. We rarely had a moment to ourselves.

One night at dinner, he surprised me with a question, "I see you have not been to the general store for a few days. Are you ready to go back into town and sell more jams and embroidery?"

I glanced to Eliza, then shook my head at Sam. "No, I don't think so. I am going to keep working on them, but I wonder if I could find another way to sell them. That is, if you don't mind me still selling them?"

Sam looked a little sheepish as he shook his head. "I don't mind at all. Not really. But here is an idea—the town fair is coming up near the end of spring, in a few month or so. I wonder if you would like to have a stall and sell them then? There is usually a big crowd, because people come from many towns over to buy and sell goods."

I felt a quick flush of pleasure. Not only was I touched that Sam was still trying to help me sell my wares, he had also mentioned the fair was at the end of summer. So did that mean he still expected me to be here? Though I had already been living in his home for more than a month, we had yet to marry because the preacher was still out of town, convalescing from his broken leg. Sam had not mentioned marriage to me since that day in the wagon, and I had also not brought it up.

"I think that sounds wonderful!" I said. "Instead of going into town every few days, maybe I can sell my whole stock at the fair, all at once. I can get started now making more jams. The spring berries are ripening, and I can make jams from them, too."

Eliza grinned at both of us. "What a marvelous idea, Sam. I expect the preacher will be back in town by then, too. So we can plan the wedding and celebrate at the fair."

At her words, Sam's face went a little stiff. "Well, we'll see about that."

Eliza and I exchanged glances. Sam was obviously still undecided about getting married, even though we had been getting along so well. I knew it was because he was not sure how to support a family, and I had been unable to convince him that I would be able to help out. Now, just when I was feeling a glimmer of hope, he had dashed it again.

Eliza sighed. "Sam, you are just being unreasonable. I know you are disappointed that your gold vein has played out, but you are a talented man, with plenty of skills. You can certainly find work as a ranchhand or handyman. Perhaps you can even find work in town, at one of the—"

Sam held up a hand, cutting her off briskly. "I appreciate what you are saying, Mother, but I do not want to work on someone else's land. This is my land, and I will find a way to keep it. I certainly do not want to work in town—what would I even do? Work in a store that belongs to someone else? That is not for me."

I sat silently, wondering what I could do to help. Sam had not asked me to leave, and that made me wonder what he truly wanted. I feared that if things did not change soon, the preacher's arrival would bring them to a head. Sam would have no reason to be waiting anymore, and he would have to make a decision.

I realized I had no idea what that decision would be.

Chapter 9

The next day, I resolved to keep my good spirits and hope. Though Sam had not committed to our marriage, he also had not said a definite no. I was hopeful, then, that his mind was turning and that he was beginning to believe that we could be happy as a family, even if he was not as successful as he had wanted to be.

It was another lovely day, so I decided to pick more fruits for my jams. The berries were ripe now, and I wanted to experiment with adding them to the cherries. I was looking forward to having some very different—and delicious—jams to sell at the fair.

As I walked towards the spot where the berry bushes were thickest, I paused to admire the beautiful flowers and lush smells rising all around me. The birds and the animals were lively and full of excitement too, it seemed, chittering and chirping and flittering here and there. The air was filled with the sights and sounds and nature, and I felt a flash of gratitude simply to be standing there. Picking up the fruit basket, I slowly walked down the hill.

I had never been to this part of Sam's land before, but Eliza had told me it was where the berries were thickest. The river flowed, bubbling over the rocks, and I felt myself calming just watching it. Surely fate had me in hand, and I would find the happiness I was meant to have. A weight flowed off my shoulders like the currents of the river, and I decided to follow the riverbanks downstream for a short while.

I walked along the water with slow footsteps, enjoying the open air and sound of the current. The house was out of sight by the time I stopped, but I was still on the ranch's land. I had never been this far, and it looked like few had, as I'd had to brush past several branches to continue my path along the river. But I was enjoying my rather adventurous walk, and did not mind a few brambles in my dress.

I came to a spot where the river dropped off a low hill, forming a waterfall in front of me. Crouching down, I let my hand touch the waters. The small fish that lived in it were agitated at my sudden intrusion, swimming in between my fingers to get away. The water was cool and refreshing, and I could feel my worries being washed away by the clear waters.

As I was pulling my hand from the water, my eyes caught on a glittering object caught in the rocks along the waterfall's base. I gathered my skirts and stepped into the water, curious what it could be. Reaching in carefully, I pulled out a yellowish rock about the size of a small strawberry. I had never seen such a beautiful object before. Smiling, I placed it inside my dress pocket and started walking back to the house. If this was what I thought, Sam will be very happy.

***

Eliza had gone to visit her sister in the next village, so no one was home but me when Sam came home for lunch. I looked up with an excited smile when Sam walked in.

"Thank you for lunch," he said, rubbing the back of his neck. I smiled as I plated his food for him. I had made a good lunch, but I hoped what I had to show him would be even better.

Sam sat down as I placed his plate on the table. He reached for the fork in front of him, then froze when he saw what was sitting next to it. The yellow stone shone in the light from the windows, and an expression both pleased and in wonder spread across his face.

"Where did you get this?" he asked, picking up the stone and turning it in his fingers.

I tried to suppress a happy smile as I said, "Oh, that? I found it at the base of the waterfall about a quarter-mile away. It was embedded into the river rocks and mud. I saw some more, too, but I did want to go in too—"

Before I could finish what I was saying, Sam had pulled me into a full bear hug, squeezing me gently in his arms.

"I can't believe this. I can't believe you found these," he said, his voice muffled and happy.

"What did I find?" I asked, pleased my hunch had played out. I had only seen gold a few times, and then it had been made into jewelry already. But the golden hue of this stone had made me think that maybe Sam's gold claim wasn't washed up after all. The feeling of his body against mine was unlike anything I had ever felt. Was this what it felt like being hugged by someone you loved?

Like you never wanted them to let go? Like you could be ever so happy with them?

Sam let me go then and held my shoulders as he looked into my eyes. "You have found gold, my darling. I had checked that pool at the base of the waterfall a few times, but had given up. My first strikes were more downstream. But now you have found a bit of gold, and I'm sure there must be more."

I grinned. "I had so hoped so, Sam," I admitted. "I wasn't sure what I was seeing, but I dearly hoped."

Laughing, Sam swung me around. "You knew all along! And you let me think you did not."

"I wanted you to have as much fun discovering the gold as I did," I said.

Sam took my hand, and I felt my stomach flutter pleasantly. Then, looking at me seriously, he said, "I love you, Alice. I have fallen in love with you the first day that I saw you. And I am ready now to admit that to you. I can take care of us, now, and can be the husband you need. If you will still have me when the preacher returns."

I was quiet for a moment. "I will indeed have you, Sam Conners. But you must know now, I would have married you even if I had not found gold."

My fingers touched his cheeks ever so gently, softly, and I loved the hardness of his mouth against mine, our lips meshing together perfectly.

"In that case, may I have the honor of kissing my future bride again?" he asked softly, touching his forehead to mine.

At that moment, the door opened suddenly, and we jumped away from each other in shock. It was only Eliza, who looked from me to Sam simultaneously, before smiling widely.

"Please don't mind me. I will just go off again," she said with a chuckle.

Sam laughed as well, "I'm glad you're home, Eliza. Alice has something to tell you!"

***

The next day, Sam and I walked upstream to the pool at the base of the waterfall where I had found the gold nugget. He stepped into the water and moved expertly among the rocks, using his pick to reach down deep into the riverbed and find two more nuggets, one larger than the one I had found.

That evening at dinner, he talked of the flow of the gold and how currents pushed it into pools. The piece I had found must have been pushed to the tops of the rocks by the push of the water. How lucky that I had chosen to go for my walk and berry-gathering on that day, as the nugget could have been later washed downstream and hidden in the sand and silt.

Then, to my surprise, he handed me one of the nuggets.

"For you," he said. "I want you to use it to buy whatever you need for your jams and embroidery. I never would have found this gold if it had not been for you."

"Sam," I said, deeply touched. "I appreciate that, truly I do. But you have given me all I need. And I really don't have to keep selling jams and handkerchiefs if you don't feel comfortable with it."

Sam smiled and shook his head slightly. Then he took both my hands in his and looked me in the eyes. "I want you to do whatever makes you happiest, Alice," he said seriously. "You have changed my life, and my mother's, and I owe you my happiness."

Glancing up at him, I smiled slightly. "Well, I would like to make a nice sampler for your mother, and I did have a new idea for jams to sell at the fair in a few weeks. But I think I will stick to berry jams for now. The apple butter is not really to my taste."

With a grin, Sam gathered me in his arms. "That sounds wonderful. Berry jam is my favorite, after all!"

Epilogue

One year later

I sat on the porch holding a cup of coffee and looking out over the fields. The spring crop was just starting to really come in, and I treasures these quiet times. Lately, they had been few and far to come by.

Feeling nostalgic, I thought back to a year ago, and how much my life had changed.

A few days after finding the gold nuggets, Sam had gone back to his claim and found a large vein running right through it. He had hired a team of men to help him work it, and even after paying them had come out quite ahead. He said he was sure there was more gold there, too.

The preacher had returned to town just before the spring fair, and Sam and I were finally wed. I had still had a few worries that he might change his mind, but as the date approached, I realized I was secure in his love. The wedding was lovely, with fresh flowers and blossoms decorating the pews.

I was happy to finally be properly wed, but it was such a busy time for a wedding! I was working to get my last jams canned and ready, and Eliza had even decided to bake some cookies and breads for the stall. We had a wonderful time and sold everything we had made. Boone even stopped by to purchase some of Eliza's bread. He had a young lady on his arm, and Sam was a bit more cordial to him this time.

"Alice!" I heard my name called. "Would you like another coffee?" I turned with a smile, seeing Eliza step out of the front door.

"I would, thank you," I said, starting to stand carefully. "Let me help you."

"Oh no, I wouldn't hear of it," she said. "You just help out by taking this little bundle. I think she is starting to wake up."

With a grin, I reached out my arms for Samantha. She was only two months old, but she already had Sam's eyes and nose. Sam, for his part, had shown himself to be a doting father, and I was looking forward to raising a family together.

As I was holding Samantha, I saw Sam heading in from the fields, in the direction I had been watching. He was riding his dark mare, which he had bought with some of the gold. After striking his claim, he had decided he wanted a little more stability, so had upgraded the farm and bought a few heads of cattle and some find horses. Ranch life agreed with him, it seemed, though he did still visit his claim from time to time, still pulling a few nuggets from it.

He said it reminded him of me, but I think I'm the one struck it rich.

The End

Please Check out My Other Works

By checking out the link below

http://cleanromancepublishing.com/fjauth

Many thanks for taking the time to buy and read through this book.

It means lots to be supported by SPECIAL readers like YOU.

Hope you enjoyed the book; please support my writing by leaving an honest review to assist other readers.

.

With Regards,

Faith Johnson